MaN
ON the RUN

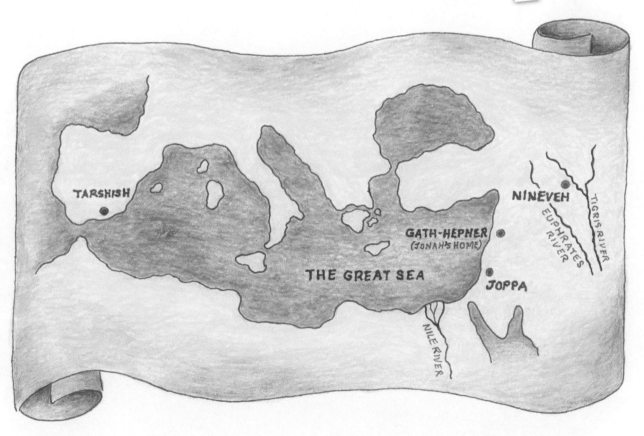

Man on the Run
Text ©2013 by Tim Augustyn
Illustrations ©2013 by Tracy R. Stern
Published by CreateSpace
    A DBA of On-Demand Publishing, LLC
    Part of the Amazon Group of companies

Based on the sermon series by Colin S. Smith: *How to Avoid a God-Centered Life* ©2009

Illustrations: Tracy R. Stern
Cover design: Anna Piro
Interior design: Anna Piro
First printing 2013
Printed in the United States of America

ISBN – 13: 978-1492753889
ISBN – 10: 1492753882

For Karis, Caleb, Clay and Kaya...

"What's that, Lord?
What did you say?
You want me to go where...
and I'm leaving today?"

"To Nineveh? No way!
I refuse to go there.
Those people are bad,
they don't even care."

"Lord, I've seen you with sinners,
seen how you behave.
They turn from their sins
and you rush in to save."

"Your anger is slow
and your love burns so bright,
but I'll never tell
even one Ninevite!"

So, off Jonah ran
from God and his plans,
taking a vacation
from his commands...

...to a ship that was headed
far, far away—
to the ends of the earth—
for he would not obey.

God sent a storm
the very next day,
and the sun disappeared,
the sky turned all grey.

He made the crew tremble.
He made the boat bend
to show that he cared
for his runaway friend.

The ship tossed and turned,
but Jonah slept well...
'til God woke him up
with a story to tell:

"This storm is my fault;
I ran from the Lord.
To make it calm down,
throw me overboard."

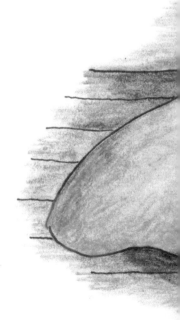

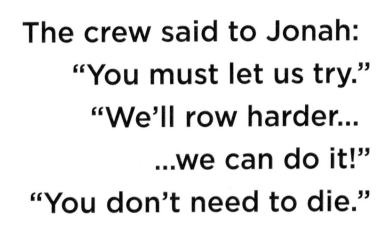

The crew said to Jonah:
"You must let us try."
"We'll row harder...
...we can do it!"
"You don't need to die."

So the brave men
boldly headed for shore,
but God blew against them
like never before.

The men cried in fear:
"She's about to go down!
Do something quick
or we're all gonna drown!"

The captain said,
"Men, lift him up high.
Throw 'em into the deep.
Only one man must die."

The satisfied wind
then quickly blew south,
leaving each of the men
with a wide-open mouth.

"We ran from you, Lord,
but your anger is slow.
You are the Captain
of every man's soul."

While down in the deep
there were two glowing eyes,
swimming toward Jonah,
mighty in size.

Do not blame fate,
the sailors, or luck.
This was the hand
of God that had struck.

"Three days and three nights
in the heart of the sea,
I found out that God does the
saving, not me!"

"I ran from you, Lord,
but your love burns so bright.
You hold the keys
when death's gate is shut tight."

Then up from the belly
Jonah suddenly rose,
a brand new man
wrapped in old, smelly clothes.

In the sand where he lay,
God's voice could be heard:
"Go now to Nineveh
and bring them my word."

A few days later,
Jonah showed up in town
with his strange accent.
Here's how it went down:

He cleared his throat
and stood up tall,
"40 more days
until Nineveh's fall!"

The people fell down.
They turned from their sin.
And God saved the whole city
from what might have been.

"We ran from you, Lord,
but your love burns so bright.
You are the King
who turns darkness to light!"

They continued to celebrate
out in the streets,
every day, every night
for what seemed like weeks.

But Jonah could not even
share in their joy,
"Lord, why did you save...
instead of destroy?"

So, Jonah complained
to God as he built
a shelter...while covered
in anger and guilt.

"Your anger's too slow
and your love burns too bright.
That's why I ran from
your plans, Lord, that night."

He awoke the next morning
to find something new.
A vine had sprung up!
It grew and it grew...

...'til Jonah forgot
about all his grief.
He smiled and smiled,
admiring his leaf.

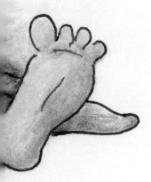

But the comfort God gave,
he now took away,
eaten up by his worm
at dawn the next day.

So there Jonah sat
with his vine-turned-to-rope
that had withered away
along with his hope.

"Jonah, my son,
how you care for this vine,
but not for these people,
although they are mine."

"Each one I planted.
Each life I gave.
Why are you angry
when I choose to save?"

"A man on the run
    from God... I was lost.
    But he never let go
    in spite of the cost."

"Now wait just a minute...
    my story's not done!
    It might not be clear
    how this points to God's Son..."

"God's anger is slow
because Jesus died.
He calmed the storm,
made it safe inside."

"God's love burns so bright,
when you run to him,
he melts all your anger
and carries your sin."

"You are a gracious God
and merciful,
slow to anger and
abounding in steadfast love,
and relenting from disaster."

JONAH 4:2 (ESV)

Made in United States
Troutdale, OR
03/05/2025